A Note for Parents and Teachers

A focus on phonics helps beginning readers gain skill and confidence with reading. Each story in the Bright Owl Books series highlights one vowel sound— for *Save the Cake!*, it's the long "a" sound. At the end of the book, you'll find two Story Starters, just for fun. Story Starters are open-ended questions that can be used as a jumping-off place for conversation, storytelling, and imaginative writing.

At Kane Press, we believe the most important part of any reading program is the shared experience of a good story. We hope you'll enjoy *Save the Cake!* with a child you love!

For information regarding permission, contact the publisher through its website: www.kanepress.com

Library of Congress Cataloging-in-Publication Data
Names: Coxe, Molly, author, illustrator.
Title: Save the cake! / by Molly Coxe.
Description: New York : Kane Press, [2019] | Series: Bright Owl books |
Summary: "Two snails, Nate and Kate, bake a cake for their grandpa but have to avoid a snake by the lake to get it to him, in this book that features the long 'a' sound"— Provided by publisher.
Identifiers: LCCN 2018028532 (print) | LCCN 2018035243 (ebook) | ISBN 9781635920994 (ebook) | ISBN 9781635920987 (pbk) | ISBN 9781635920970 (reinforced library binding)
Subjects: | CYAC: Birthday cakes—Fiction. | Parties—Fiction. | Snails—Fiction. | Snakes—Fiction. | Humorous stories.
Classification: LCC PZ7.C839424 (ebook) | LCC PZ7.C839424 Sav 2019 (print) | DDC [E]—dc23
LC record available at https://lccn.loc.gov/201802853

10 9 8 7 6 5 4 3 2 1

First published in the United States of America in 2019 by Kane Press, Inc.
Printed in China

Book Design: Michelle Martinez

Bright Owl Books is a registered trademark of Kane Press, Inc.

Visit us online at www.kanepress.com

 Like us on Facebook
facebook.com/kanepress

 Follow us on Twitter
@KanePress

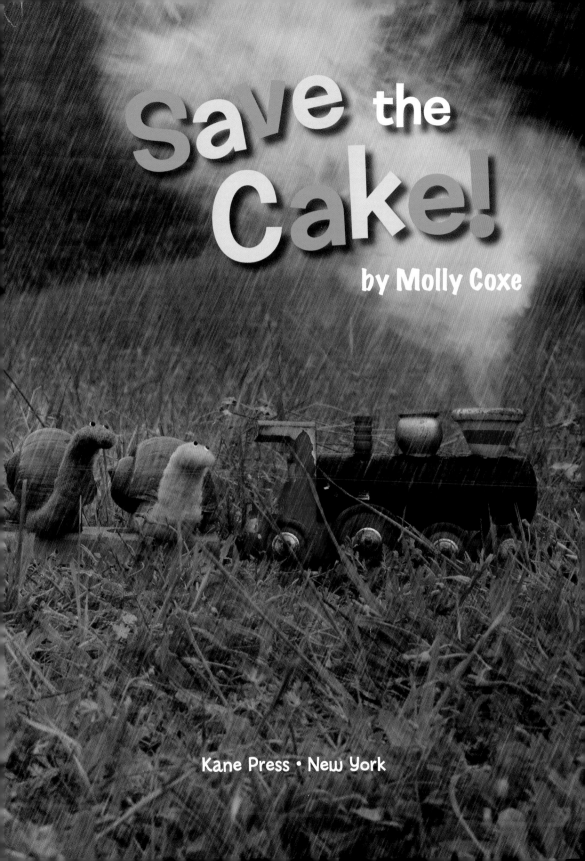

Save the Cake!

by Molly Coxe

Kane Press • New York

Kate and Nate
bake a cake
for Grandpa Jake.
It takes all day.

Kate and Nate
place the cake
on a plate
in some hay.

They take the trail
around the lake.
"Hurry, Nate!" says Kate.
"We will be late!"

"Wait!" says Nate.
"A snake is on the trail!"

"Do snakes like cake?"
Kate asks.
"Maybe," says Nate.
"Let's take the train
around the lake."

Kate and Nate
race to the train.
They are too late.

"Let's take a plane
to Grandpa Jake's,"
says Kate.

Kate and Nate
race to the plane.
They are too late.

"Let's sail across the lake,"
says Nate.

Nate and Kate set sail.

It starts to rain.
"Save the cake!"
says Kate.

Nate and Kate
get the cake
out of the rain.
"Nate! The snake went away,"
says Kate.
"Hooray!" says Nate.

Kate and Nate
take the trail
to Grandpa Jake's.

"Sorry we are late,"
says Kate.
"It's okay,"
says Grandpa Jake.
"We are still waiting
for Snake."

"For Snake?" says Nate.
"The snake by the lake?"
"The same!" says Grandpa Jake.
"Snake is my great mate!"

Snake makes his way
to Grandpa Jake's.
He brings daisies in a vase,
a game to play,
and a pair of skates.

"You are just in time for cake!"
say Nate and Kate.
"Happy birthday, Jake!"
says Snake.

Story Starters

Gail is a snail.
Tell a tale
about Gail.

It is Snake's birthday.
What games
will they play?